An Itch To Scratch

With love to Rachel, Laura and Deanna –
the best back scratchers!
D.H.

For Matthew and Georgie
L.C.

First published in Great Britain in 2005 by
Gullane Children's Books
an imprint of Pinwheel Limited
Winchester House, 259-269 Old Marylebone Road,
London NW1 5XJ

1 3 5 7 9 10 8 6 4 2

Text © Damian Harvey 2005
Illustrations © Lynne Chapman 2005

The right of Damian Harvey and Lynne Chapman to be identified as the author and illustrator of this work
has been asserted by them in accordance with the Copyright, Designs, and Patents Act, 1988.
A CIP record for this title is available from the British Library.

ISBN 1-86233-454-4

Printed and bound in China

An Itch To Scratch

Damian Harvey

illustrated by **Lynne Chapman**

GULLANE
CHILDREN'S BOOKS

Big Gorilla had an itch.
It was right in the
middle of his back.

He wriggled

and he squirmed,

he reached

and he stretched.

But he
just couldn't
find the spot.

He danced round the room,
scritching and scratching.
He bumped into a boulder,
and knocked over a log.
But he still couldn't find the itch.

Mother Gorilla frowned and said,
"You need a scratching tree,
it's just the thing when
I have an itch. Now go away
before you wake the baby."

So Big Gorilla wandered off to find a tree.
He wriggled and he
rubbed, he scritched
and he scratched.

But...

. . . the tree was all **gummy** and it stuck to his fur. And his itch was worse than before.

"It might be the thing for you," said Big Gorilla, "but it's definitely not for me."

"You should wallow in
the mud," said Warthog,
with a grunt.
"It's just the thing
for a hog with an *itch*."

So Big Gorilla found some mud.
He wallowed and he squelched,
he scritched and he scratched.

But...

. . . the mud was too **sloppy**.
And it went in his ears.
And it went in his eyes.
And his *itch* was worse than before.

"It might be the thing for a hog," said Big Gorilla, "but it's definitely not for me."

"You should try rolling in the grass," said Lion. "It's just the thing for a lion with an *itch*."

So Big Gorilla found some grass.
He rolled and he tumbled,
he scritched **and he** scratched.

But...

. . . the grass was too *tickly*
and it stuck to his back.
   And his *itch* was
worse than before.

"It might be the thing for
a lion," said Big Gorilla,
"but it's definitely not for me."

"You should try rubbing against an old anthill," said Elephant. "It's just the thing for an elephant with an *itch*."

So Big Gorilla found an anthill.
He leaned
    and he rubbed,
he scritched
    and he scratched.

Then he scritched
and he scratched
some more.

But...

. . . the anthill he'd found wasn't
old at all, it was home to an army of ants!
They bit him and nipped him
and chased him around.

And his itch was worse than before.

"It might be the thing for an elephant," said Big Gorilla, as he ran away, "but it's definitely not for me."

Big Gorilla raced down to
the river and jumped right in.
He splished and he splashed,
he scritched and he scratched.

Then wearily
walked back home.

He washed off
the ants and the
mud and the gum.

He was tired
and wet as he
flopped on
his bed.

my dad

And the itch?
It was worse
than before!

"Look what you've done,"
said Mother Gorilla.
"You've woken our son."
Baby Gorilla dashed
from his bed and
jumped on his
dad's back.

He wriggled and tickled.
And he scritched and he scratched.
And Big Gorilla opened his eyes.